To Jon, Franny, and Henry.
And to the goat who stole my underpants
when I was three. I forgive you.—A.R.

To my mom and dad,
Thank you for the paper and crayons!
And thank you for believing in me.—M.R.

Text copyright © 2019 by Abigail Rayner.
Illustrations copyright © 2019 by Molly Ruttan.
First published in the United States, Great Britain, Canada, Australia, and New Zealand in 2019
by NorthSouth Books, Inc., an imprint of NordSüd Verlag AG, CH-8050 Zürich, Switzerland.

Distributed in the United States by NorthSouth Books, Inc., New York 10016.
Library of Congress Cataloging-in-Publication Data is available.
ISBN: 978-0-7358-4289-2 (trade edition)

1 3 5 7 9 · 10 8 6 4 2
Printed in Latvia, by Livonia Print, Riga, 2019.
www.northsouth.com

FSC
www.fsc.org
MIX
Paper from
responsible sources
FSC® C002795

I AM A THIEF!

by **Abigail Rayner**

illustrated by **Molly Ruttan**

North South

I am a thief.
Me. Eliza Jane Murphy.
Line Leader. Caring Friend.
Captain of the
Worm Rescue Team.

THIEF!

The stone
made me do it.
It sparkled at me.

In a flash of
brilliant green
it was . . .

MINE!

And my heart . . .

Stopped singing.

My letters went wonky.

I was too heavy
to swing.

Everyone stopped what
they were doing and
looked for the stone.
My cheeks burned!
I wanted to put it back . . .
But what if someone saw?

At home, I hid it.
But I felt like I glowed green.

"Mama, have you ever
stolen anything?"
Mama smiled. "A magnet."
"Did you give it back?"
"Of course. Why?"
I shrugged.

My own mother! A thief!

"Grandpa, have you ever stolen anything?"
Grandpa chuckled.
"I once took a Yankees keychain from my friend Bill."
        "Did he find out?"
        "He did. By golly was he mad!"

AND Grandpa George?
And why was he laughing?

Who else in my family was a thief?
I decided to investigate.

Nana Iris admitted
to taking packets
of sugar
from the diner.

Often!

AND her dog James was a notorious
sausage thief.

My baby brother Jack once swiped a lady's sandwich.

Two Christmases ago, Cousin Clara stole Santa's beard.

Well, she tried anyway.

And Uncle Tim's goat pinched Jack's underpants.

And ate them.

It seemed like everyone in my family was a thief.

Maybe I should have felt better,
knowing I wasn't alone . . .

But I didn't.

I knew what I had to do.

The next day
I gave back the stone.
Ms. Delano did not send
me to the principal,
or say my days as line
leader were finished.

She said I was . . .

BRAVE?

I told Ms. Delano I came from
a long line of thieves.
She had probably stolen something, too,
if she thought about it.

Then I realized.
Nobody is *just* a thief.

Everyone is a lot of things!

We put the stone back.

And my heart
started singing again.

I decided to close my investigation.

But it turned out, it wasn't *quite* finished . . .

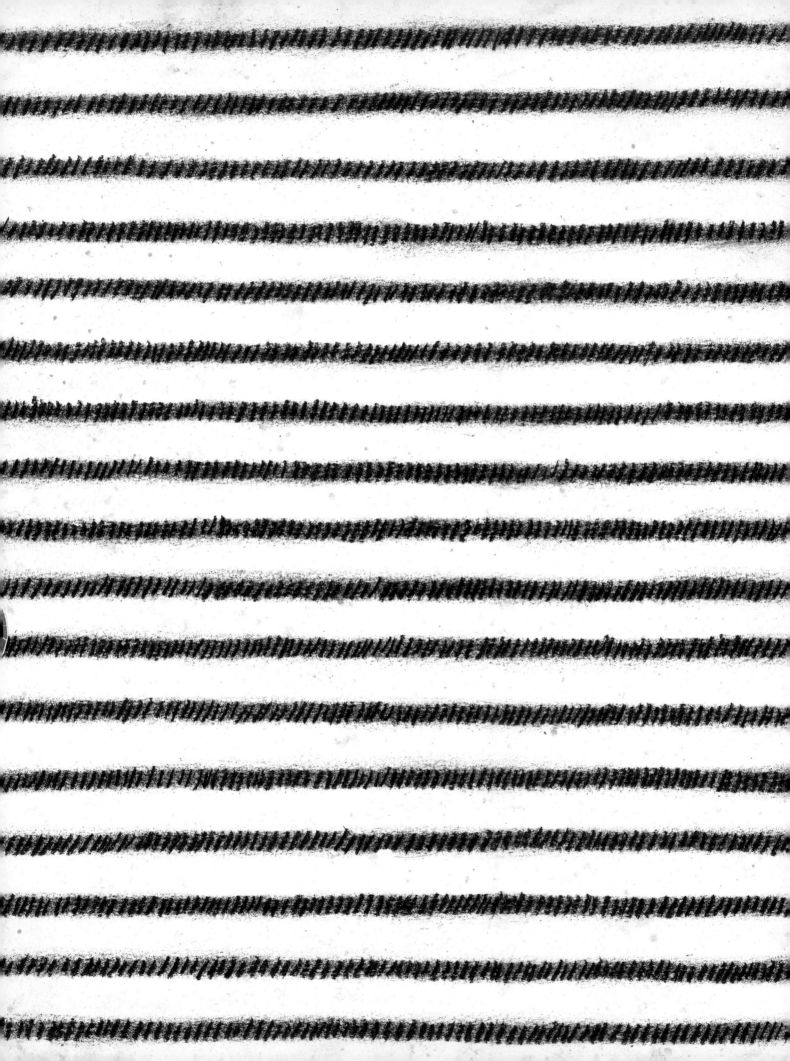